David Fickling Books presents

LIONHEART

RICHARD COLLINGRIDGE

To Archie and Haydn

David Fickling Books

"There can't be.
There can't be.
There's no such thing
as monsters."

But what was that sound?

Richard hugged his
Lionheart tightly.

Something was there
and Richard was scared.

So he ran . . .

He ran and he ran,
through the streets
and over the hills,
through the forest
and into the fields.

But he was being chased . . .

All around him the grass grew thick, and turned into sticks,
and the sticks grew tall, and turned into trees,

but still he was being chased . . .

so Richard kept running.

Until he ran into

a magical jungle . . .

. . . where there were
animals all around.

Some big, some small,
Some thin, some tall,
Some mean, some hairy,
Some fat, some scary.

But Richard couldn't stay to look.

The monster was coming . . .

so Richard kept running.

He ran and he ran

until . . .

He ran into something . . .

or someone!

It was Lionheart!
But he wasn't a toy anymore.

"Come with me!"
his Lionheart said.
And Richard went.

Away from the monster.
Away from his fears.

Together they jumped over the pointing rocks

and went under the falling water.

They travelled deep, deep,
deep into the Lost City
where Richard played
with the animals.

And he was having
so much fun that
he forgot the monster.

He forgot he was scared.

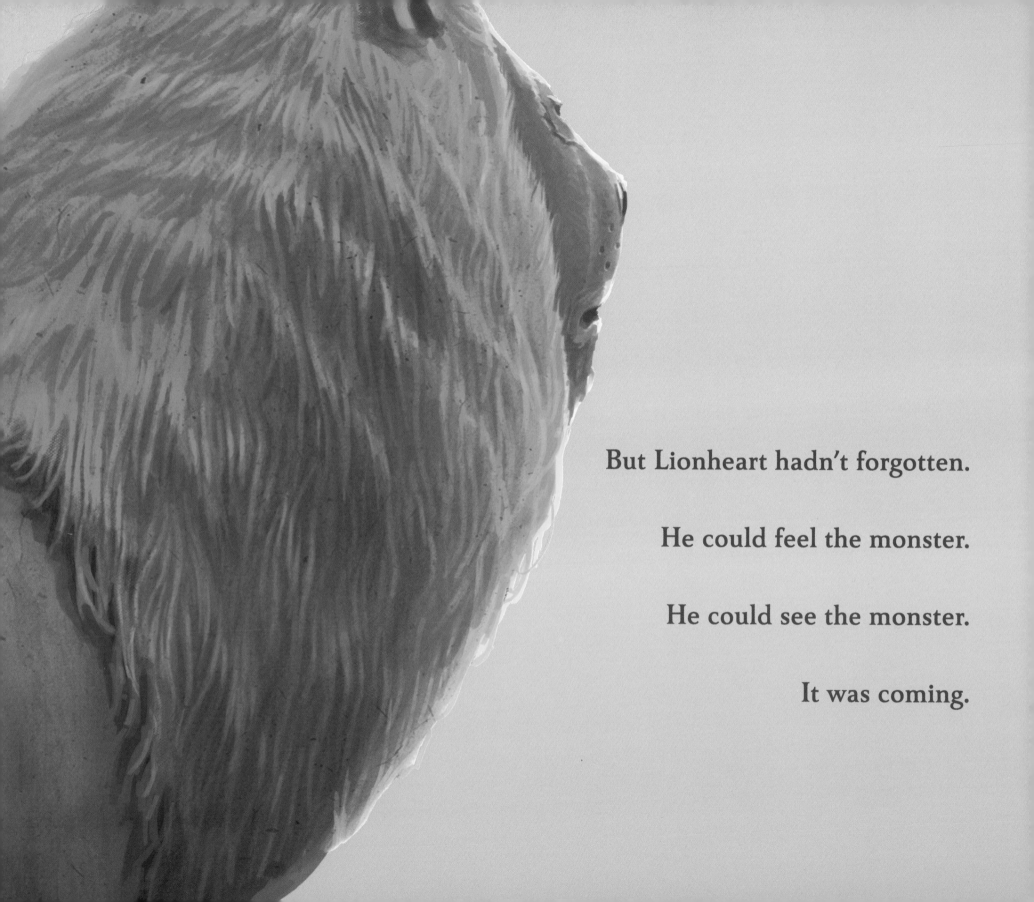

But Lionheart hadn't forgotten.

He could feel the monster.

He could see the monster.

It was coming.

The animals saw it too and they were scared.

Then Richard saw it!

But when Richard
looked at Lionheart
he knew what
to do. He knew
how to be brave —
his Lionheart
had shown him.

So together they
took a deep breath
and started to . . .

ROAR!

They roared SO loudly that the monster and all of Richard's fears

And Richard wasn't afraid of monsters anymore.